Wonderful Qualities I See in You

_____

_____

_____

_____

My Hopes and Dreams for Your Life

_____

_____

_____

_____

A Sweet Melody of God's Love for Me

Mama, Sing My Song

An Imprint of Thomas Nelson

written by
Amanda Seibert

illustrated by
Sally Garland

Published in Nashville, Tennessee, by Tommy Nelson. Tommy Nelson is an imprint of Thomas Nelson. Thomas Nelson is a registered trademark of HarperCollins Christian Publishing, Inc.

Tommy Nelson titles may be purchased in bulk for educational, business, fund-raising, or sales promotional use. For information, please email SpecialMarkets@ThomasNelson.com.

"One Very Wonderful You," ℗ Amanda Seibert, written by Amanda Seibert, performed by Praytell and Mama Sing My Song, MP3 audio, 3:10, 2022.

Scripture quotations are taken from the Holy Bible, New Living Translation. Copyright © 1996, 2004, 2015 by Tyndale House Foundation. Used by permission of Tyndale House Publishers, Carol Stream, Illinois 60188. All rights reserved.

ISBN 978-1-4002-3555-1 (audiobook)
ISBN 978-1-4002-3556-8 (eBook)
ISBN 978-1-4002-3554-4 (HC)

Library of Congress Cataloging-in-Publication Data

Names: Seibert, Amanda, 1985- author. | Garland, Sally Anne, illustrator.
Title: Mama, sing my song : a sweet melody of God's love for me / Amanda Seibert ; illustrated by Sally Garland.
Description: Nashville, Tennessee : Thomas Nelson, 2022. | Audience: Ages 4-8 | Summary: "In this meaningful picture book for 4- to 8-year-olds, adorable children of all kinds are reminded through each mother's song that they are uniquely created by a loving God. He writes a child's song into the fabric of the universe and sings of our purpose and His great love for us"-- Provided by publisher.
Identifiers: LCCN 2022008954 (print) | LCCN 2022008955 (ebook) | ISBN 9781400235544 (h/c) | ISBN 9781400235551 (audiobook) | ISBN 9781400235568 (ebook)
Subjects: LCSH: God (Christianity)--Love--Juvenile literature. | Mother and child--Religious aspects--Christianity--Juvenile literature.
Classification: LCC BT140 .S45 2022 (print) | LCC BT140 (ebook) | DDC 242/.62--dc23/eng/20220322
LC record available at https://lccn.loc.gov/2022008954
LC ebook record available at https://lccn.loc.gov/2022008955

Written by Amanda Seibert
Illustrated by Sally Garland

Printed in South Korea

22 23 24 25 26 SAM 6 5 4 3 2 1

Mfr: SAM / Seoul, South Korea / August 2022 / PO #12040398

For the Lord your God is living among you.

He is a *mighty* savior.

He will take delight in you with gladness.

With his love, he will *calm* all your fears.

He will *rejoice* over you with *joyful songs*.

—ZEPHANIAH 3:17

To Jane, Owen, and Will, who make my heart sing.

—LOVE, MAMA

For Johnny.

—SG

Did you know there's a song for each child on earth
about how much you're loved and how much you're worth?
A song to remind you that you always belong—

Oh, Mama, Mama,

will you sing my song?

Snuggle up, darling. Now sit close and listen
to my favorite song that has ever been written!
A song so amazing, delightful, and true—
a marvelous song about marvelous *you!*

My beautiful child,
you are one of a kind,
perfectly made,
and uniquely designed.

You're a masterpiece—God's work of art
with His joy in your smile and His love in your heart.

The very same God who *painted the skies*
gave you your giggle and the spark in your eyes.

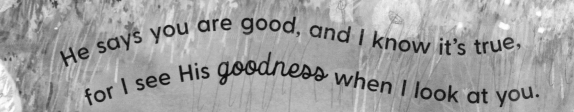

He says you are good, and I know it's true, for I see His *goodness* when I look at you.

In the whole wide world, all the way to the moon,

God made just one *very wonderful* you!

You're dearly loved, and I hope you see

what a *special* treasure you are to me.

Do you ever worry that you're not *enough*
or that all of your trying just won't measure up?

Remember that God makes all things new,
and He's making *beautiful* things out of you.

When you feel alone in the darkness of night,
God's right beside you, and He'll be *your light*.

Just like a shepherd watching over his lamb,
He's holding you *safely* in His loving hands.

'Cause in the whole wide world, all the way to the moon,

God made just *one* very wonderful you!

You're *dearly loved*, and I hope you see what a special treasure you are to me.

But I'm not the only one singing your song—
there's One who's been singing over you *all along*.
From morning to evening and all through the night,
God sings this to you with *joy* and *delight* . . .

In the whole wide world, all the way *to the moon,*

nothing could keep Me from loving you!

'Cause you're My child, and I hope you see what a special treasure you are to Me.

Oh, Mama, Mama,

could it really be true?

Does God really love me

the way that you do?

As much as I love you, my dear, it's a fact:

God loves you a million times more than that!

From the top of your head to your wiggly toes,

whatever you do and wherever you go,

as deep as the sea, as high as the stars,

forever and ever, just as you are.

And when you remember God's big love for you,

don't forget, darling, that I love you too!

I promise you this, for my whole life long,

I'll always be here for you, singing your song.

The Special Meaning of Your Name

_____

_____

_____

_____

A Word or Verse I Speak over Your Life

_____

_____

_____

_____